W9-AUS-469

LILY

TO THE RESCUE

TWO LITTLE
PIGGIES

W. BRUCE CAMERON

LILY
TO THE rescue

TWO LITTLE PIGGIES

Illustrations by

JENNIFER L. MEYER

SCHOLASTIC INC.

No part of this publication may be reproduced, stored in a retrieval system,
or transmitted in any form or by any means, electronic, mechanical,
photocopying, recording, or otherwise, without written permission of the
publisher. For information regarding permission, write to Starscape,
an imprint of Tom Doherty Associates, an imprint of Macmillan
Publishing Group, LLC, 120 Broadway, New York, NY 10271.

ISBN 978-1-338-83117-7

Copyright © 2020 by W. Bruce Cameron. Illustrations © 2020 by
Jennifer L. Meyer. All rights reserved. Published by Scholastic Inc.,
557 Broadway, New York, NY 10012, by arrangement with Starscape,
an imprint of Tom Doherty Associates. SCHOLASTIC and associated logos
are trademarks and/or registered trademarks of Scholastic Inc.

The publisher does not have any control over and does not assume any
responsibility for author or third-party websites or their content.

1 2021

Printed in the U.S.A.   23

This edition first printing, January 2022

For my friends who are working to save them all

at Best Friends Animal Society.

LILY
TO THE rescue

TWO LITTLE
PIGGIES

1

Snow had melted, the birds were in the trees, and I was in the backyard playing ball with my girl, Maggie Rose, her older brother Bryan, and her even older brother Craig.

What a great day! Craig would throw the ball at Bryan, who would try to hit it with a big wooden stick. If he missed, I would run after the ball and grab it and then carry it to

Maggie Rose because I am a good dog who makes sure that everyone gets to play.

When it was Craig's turn to hit the ball, it sometimes went over the fence and into the trees beyond. If that happened, Maggie Rose would open the gate, and I would sniff out where the ball had gone.

The grasses were long and fragrant, full of their own odors, which made it difficult to find the scent of the ball. I had help, though, because there was a crow who was playing with us. His name was Casey, and he was my friend.

I first met Casey at a dog park. He had a wing that did not work well. Then he lived at Work for a little while. (More about Work later.) Now both of his wings are very strong, and he can fly wherever he wants. Some of the time, he wants to fly to where I am for a visit, which I like very much.

Whenever I dashed out of the gate, I looked up into the trees to see where Casey had flown. Usually, Casey chose a branch very close to where the ball lay in the tangle of weeds and shrubs. If I followed Casey, I would get close enough to the ball to catch the scent trail it made as it bounced into the woods. Then, of course, finding it was easy.

I always jumped on the ball and played with it a bit, throwing it up in the air and catching it for myself, because I am a dog who knows how to add extra fun to a game. Then I trotted back to the gate where Maggie

Rose was waiting. I would give her the ball because, as I mentioned, I am a good dog.

Maggie Rose would carry the ball over and hand it to one of her brothers. That disappointed me. When Maggie Rose threw the ball, I could usually catch it on the bounce and then we could really have fun, playing Chase-Me. When Craig or Bryan threw, it was a lot more work to chase the ball down.

"Hey," Craig called to Maggie Rose. "Want a turn at bat?"

I glanced at Maggie Rose curiously. She suddenly seemed a little shy and scared. What had Craig said to her?

"No," she said in a small voice.

"Why not? Come on, give it a try," Craig told her.

Maggie Rose shrugged. "I can't hit it hard. I'm just a runt," she said. Her voice was very quiet.

Craig went up to her with a frown on

his face. He looked at Bryan. "Good going, Bryan," Craig said.

"How is this *my* fault?" Bryan replied.

"You're the one who always calls her a runt," Craig accused.

I went over to Craig, who had the ball. I did Sit so that he would know I was ready to play the game some more. Maybe they had stopped playing because they believed I might not be prepared.

"Well," Bryan replied, "she *is* a runt. She's the shortest girl in the third grade."

Craig frowned at Bryan and then turned back to his sister. "Don't listen to him, Maggie Rose," he said. "You're not a runt." I nosed Maggie Rose's leg because she still seemed a little sad. "Besides, Bryan's the shortest boy in the fifth grade."

"Am not!" Bryan cried.

"Are, too. Come on," Craig said to Maggie Rose. "Take a turn at bat." Craig walked a few steps away from my girl and turned. I sat right next to Maggie Rose. Bryan held out the stick, and Maggie Rose took it from him. She bit her lip and stood with the stick on her shoulder, facing Craig.

Bryan went behind Maggie Rose. "Here," he said. "Choke up on the bat a little." He reached out and moved my girl's hands so that they were higher up on the stick. "That's it."

I wagged because it seemed that something fun was about to happen. I noticed that Casey had soared out of the trees and was watching from his perch on the fence.

"Okay," Craig said to Maggie Rose, "keep your eye on the ball!" Craig gently tossed the ball in our direction. I was about to jump up for it, and it's a good thing I didn't, because Maggie Rose chopped at the air with her stick. The ball bounced into the heavy glove Bryan wore on his hand.

"Strike one!" Bryan called.

"We're not doing strikes right now, Bryan," Craig said.

"No," Maggie Rose said. "He can do strikes." She looked and sounded stubborn. "I want to play with the real rules."

Bryan threw the ball back to Craig. I hoped Craig would drop it and I could chase it. Wasn't that the point of all of this, me chasing the ball?

"Here it comes, Maggie Rose!" Craig called. Maggie Rose tensed. I tensed, too. Craig threw the ball, and it landed on the ground past my girl, and Bryan grabbed it before I could.

This wasn't how we were supposed to be playing the game!

"Strike two!" Maggie Rose called.

"Three strikes and you're out, Maggie Rose," Bryan said as he threw the ball back to Craig.

"Okay," Craig said encouragingly, "third one's a charm!"

Craig carefully moved his hand and the ball sailed through the air and my girl swung her stick and there was a loud thud. She hit it! The ball bounced into the dirt, moving very slowly.

"Run to first base!" Craig called. "Hurry, Maggie Rose!"

Maggie Rose dropped the stick and started to run toward a tree, and I had to make a decision. Bryan was chasing the ball, which

had not gone very far and was already slow-
ing to a stop. On the other hand, my girl was
running, and I loved to run with her.

But I felt that we were still playing ball!
So I dashed past Bryan and leaped on it.

"No!" Bryan bellowed.

No? No what? How did *no* apply to a wonderful situation like this?

"Run to second base!" Craig yelled.

My girl slapped the tree. She switched
direction and started running toward a spot
on the fence behind Craig. Bryan made to

grab the ball from me, and I took off. We were playing Chase-Me! I love this game!

"No, Lily!" Bryan called. "Come here!"

Maggie Rose touched the fence.

"Keep running, Maggie Rose!" Craig cheered. "Go to third, go to third!"

Bryan was still chasing me. Craig can catch me, but Bryan could run all day and all night and he would never be able to get the ball from me. I darted happily around, with Bryan lunging and grabbing and missing.

Maggie Rose jumped on a flat rock with both feet.

"Go home!" Craig shouted happily. He was laughing. "You're going to make it, Maggie Rose!"

Part of what is fun about Chase-Me is letting another dog or a person have the ball sometimes so that the game can reverse and become Chase in the other direction. I bowed with my front legs flat on the ground and my rump high in the air. The ball dropped out of my mouth and bounced between my front paws.

Bryan rushed up and threw himself forward, landing and sliding in the dirt. He picked up the ball!

Bryan ran at Maggie Rose, and I bounded joyfully after him. As he ran, the ball in his hand swung back and forth, and I wanted him to know that I knew we were playing the game of Chase-Bryan-with-the-Ball, so I jumped up to try to grab it from him. Bryan tripped over me and sprawled in the dirt.

"Hurry, Maggie Rose!" Craig called.

Maggie Rose was running as fast as she could, heading back to where she had dropped the stick.

Panting, Bryan stumbled to his feet, his shoes digging into the dirt as he ran at my girl.

"Safe!" Craig yelled. He bounded over and picked up Maggie Rose and swung her around and around, laughing.

Bryan turned and threw the ball with all

his might at the fence. It bounced a few times on the way there, hit the fence, and I caught it in midair!

This game was the best!

The back door of the house slid open, and Mom leaned out. "Maggie Rose? Boys? Would you like to go with me to save some baby pigs?" she called.

Car ride! Craig sat up in the front next to Mom, and I sat in the back with Maggie Rose and Bryan. They smelled deliciously sweaty in their T-shirts.

"Where are the pigs, Mom? Are we going to a farm?" Craig asked.

Mom shook her head. "No," she replied. "It's the strangest thing. I just got the call. It may even be a hoax. They said there are two baby pigs running around inside a truck stop off the highway. It doesn't seem very likely, but that's what they said."

"What's a hoax?" Maggie Rose asked.

"It's kind of a joke that involves someone telling a lie," Mom replied.

"Well, then," Maggie Rose said, "I hope it's not a hoax because I'd love to see some little piglets. Can I name them, Mom?"

"We'll see," Mom answered.

"If they're boy pigs, then Craig and I should name them," Bryan declared.

"We'll see," Mom repeated.

I wagged because I smelled wonderful things outside the car, things like dogs and trees and horses and other animals. Wherever we were going was probably going to be a lot of fun!

We drove long enough for me to become drowsy in the back seat and fall asleep with my head on Bryan's shoulder. When he said, "Lily, quit breathing on me," I woke up a little and licked his ear. Everyone but Bryan laughed, so I did it again.

Bryan had eaten a peanut butter sandwich earlier, and I could taste it on his ear, which I thought was simply amazing. Why don't all people put peanut butter in their ears? It seemed a very smart thing to do.

I licked Bryan's ear again, and he pushed my face away.

Finally, we arrived at a hot place where the ground was covered with hard cement and the grass and trees were in the distance. Nearby, cars and trucks large and small roared up and down a very busy road.

"Okay, everyone," Mom said. "Stay close to me. I don't know what we're dealing with here."

We walked up to some glass doors, and

when they slid open, a
gust of cold air brought me
delicious food scents: melted cheese; broiling hot dogs; sweet, sticky drinks in cans
and cups.

There was something else as well: two
animals I had never smelled before. There
were animals inside this place!

A large man walked up to greet us. He

smelled a little like meat and a little like plastic. "Are you from the animal rescue?" he asked.

"Yes," Mom replied. "What's this about some pigs?"

The man shrugged. "I was just sitting behind the cash register and the doors opened, and these two pigs came walking in as happy as you please. They're pretty young, these pigs, but they're fast. I tried chasing them—no luck."

The animal smell was coming from something called *pigs*.

"Mom, can I have a candy bar?" Craig asked.

"Me, too!" Bryan said.

"Let's just figure out what we have first, boys. Sir, where are the pigs now?" Mom asked.

"I reckon they're in the back somewhere, probably underneath the sweatshirt rack. That's where I saw them last. I'm a little too old to be chasing critters on my hands and knees."

"All right," Mom said. "Bryan and Craig, you boys start checking up and down the aisles and see if you can spot the pigs. Maggie Rose, you stay with Lily."

I knew the word *Stay* but had never been

fond of it. It meant I should not move until I was told I was a good dog. Sometimes I didn't even get a treat for doing Stay, which was very unfair.

Lily put her hand on my collar and told me to Sit, so I sat. I watched curiously as Mom, Craig, and Bryan crept through this big place.

There was food—I could still smell it—but they didn't seem interested in that. I didn't know why. Instead, they were pushing through big metal racks with pieces of soft cloth hanging from them. They also looked intently at the floor, but there were no treats there.

"I see them!" Craig called.

I watched, completely baffled, as Craig suddenly dropped out of view. A rack of clothing fell over, and I heard a squealing noise. It was an animal sound, and it sounded afraid.

Crash! A shelf with hats collapsed. The big man standing with us groaned quietly.

"They're coming your way, Bryan!" Craig shouted.

I started in amazement when I saw the flash of two pale animals dart across a clear space on the floor. They were both smaller than I was, but very quick. They ran a little bit like dogs, using all four legs. Obviously, these were the pigs!

"I missed!" Bryan yelled. He staggered back, and a cardboard box with bags of nuts hanging from it toppled and fell to the floor. I wagged, thinking that if my friend Casey the crow were here, he would appreciate this. He likes nuts more than just about anything.

All of a sudden, Mom knelt down. Then she stood up, shaking her head. "They just ran right past me, too. They're so fast and wiggly!"

I watched as Bryan and Craig careened

around. Some-
times I caught
a glimpse of the
two pale little
creatures as they
dashed from side to
side. This was fun!
I didn't understand
any of it, but it was
fun!

"All right, boys," Mom
called. "This is obviously
not working. Come on
back."

"Mom," Maggie Rose

said, "maybe we should let Lily see if she can make friends with them."

The boys came slouching up.

"Can I have a candy bar now, Mom?" Craig asked.

"I'll give you both candy bars for free if you'll help put the displays back once we've caught the pigs," the man standing with us said.

Both boys brightened, and I glanced at them curiously. People do things all the time that dogs don't particularly understand, but that doesn't mean it's okay not to pay attention. Right now, Bryan and Craig were alert and happy, though as far as I could see, nothing had changed.

I felt my girl's hand releasing my collar. I shook, yawning, ready for whatever we were going to do next. Now I realized why the boys had suddenly become happy. They knew Maggie Rose was going to let me go!

"Okay, Lily," Maggie Rose said. "Go tell the piggies that they should stop running away."

I heard my name but did not know what my girl was asking me to do. I sat. Doing Sit is one of the first tricks I learned, and it remains one of my most popular.

Then, a movement caught my eye. Underneath a hanging shirt, a pale snout was poking out, sniffing vigorously. I got up and looked at Maggie Rose to see if it was okay for me to stop doing Sit.

She smiled, so I knew that it was. Curious, I trotted down the aisle to take a look. I half expected Maggie Rose to call me back, but she said nothing.

I've learned that some animals are afraid of dogs, even an easygoing dog like me. So, as I got closer to the pig, I began moving more slowly and carefully. I didn't want to startle it.

I saw that my scent had reached that snout because suddenly the nose turned in my direction, twitching and snorting. The little animal poked its face all the way out and stared at me.

My nose and eyes told me several things. First, I had never smelled creatures like this before! They smelled magnificent. A heavy, earthy odor clung to them, along with a mix of other scents that included, oddly, milk.

Second, as the other one poked its head

out at me, I realized they were sisters. There is just something about the common smell of littermates. It doesn't matter if they are dogs or cats or strange four-legged creatures like these pigs. You can always tell.

These two pigs were nearly identical in every way, except that one of them had a small dark patch under one eye. And I could tell they were young. Older and bigger animals are usually slow. These two were twitching and jumping, and their heads and eyes were moving quickly to take everything in. I knew they were babies.

There are some things I understand, and one of them is that for any sort of baby, whether it be a bunny or a kitten or a pig, to be away from its mother is sad. It's not how things should be.

Something bad had happened to these pig sisters.

Or *was* happening.

3

The two pigs were staring at me, and I was staring at them. I was wagging as I drew near, being very friendly. They were not wagging, but that didn't mean anything. Casey is a very friendly crow, but he has never wagged a tail, not even when Maggie Rose feeds him a peanut.

I decided that they had so much energy I could risk a little movement. I bowed. Then I jumped up, then bowed again.

The two animals understood me! They knew that bowing meant playtime. They surged out from underneath that shirt and leaped on me, squealing and then running around in tight circles. They wanted to play Chase-Me!

I love Chase-Me whether there's a ball involved or not. I decided that the pigs should run after me first. I turned and galloped down in front of some cold glass doors, my feet skittering a little bit on the slick floor.

"Good dog, Lily!" I heard Mom call.

The little creatures came after me. They were fast! I sped up around the corner, looking back over my shoulder. They were both scampering after me at top speed.

I turned another corner, sliding precariously, almost falling, and found myself running right toward Mom and Maggie Rose and her brothers. They were all kneeling. I practically crashed into Craig, my claws

scrabbling for purchase.

A moment later, the two pigs came charging around the corner after me. When they spotted everyone on their knees, they tried to stop, but they were sliding just as I had done, and they couldn't help but skid straight into the arms of Mom and Craig and Bryan.

The pigs were not happy and were twisting and squealing, but the boys and Mom had their arms wrapped around them and hugged them tightly.

"Good job!" the man said.

"We'll be right back to help you put your displays up," Craig said.

Maggie Rose grabbed my collar. We all went back out into the sunshine. Mom put the little creatures into a cage in the very back of the truck.

"Good dog," Maggie Rose praised. "You're a good rescue dog today, Lily."

We sat in the truck with the pigs in the back while Craig and Bryan returned to the cool building again and came out a little while later with sweet-smelling candies in their hands. They gave one to Maggie Rose but did not offer any to me because dogs aren't allowed to eat that kind of thing. My girl gave me a chicken treat, which is better, anyway.

On the way home, the little animals were very anxious at first, darting back and forth in their cage. After a while, they collapsed in a heap in the corner of the cage, exhausted.

"How old are the pigs, Mom?" Bryan asked.

"It's hard to say," Mom replied. "But I doubt they can be on their own yet. We'll have to bottle-feed them."

"Do we have pig's milk to feed them?" Craig asked.

"No," Mom admitted, "but we have goat's milk. Goat's milk has a lot of fat in it, and that's what these little girls need right now."

I twisted around to put my paws on the back of the seat, peering into the cage at the two little pigs sleeping in their heap, their small chests rising and falling together. I breathed their scents deeply, drinking them in, learning pig. From now on, this odor would be known to me as the *smell of pigs*.

But there was more to them than that—there was another odor, a complex one, on their skin. I had first noticed this strong smell when I'd followed my family into the cool building.

It was pig, just like the little sisters, but

with a stronger, oily odor, one that was also touched with the faint smell of what was definitely milk. At some time not long ago, these two small pigs had been very close to a bigger, older, milky pig.

The pigs were still asleep when Mom carried their cage into Work. Work is a place with a lot of animals inside it—other dogs, cats, birds, sometimes squirrels. Now Work had two pigs. That was exciting!

I sat in the car with Maggie Rose and the boys, wagging hard and hoping I'd get to go into Work with the pigs and Mom. Lots of times I do get to go there, but not now. Mom came back into the car without the cage or the pigs, and we drove home.

We got out of the car, and I saw Casey sitting on the fence, watching us.

"Ree-ree," Casey croaked. Casey can make noises that sound like talking, and

Ree-ree is often what he says when he sees me, as if he is saying *Lily*. I wagged at him. He probably was wondering when we were going to play ball some more.

I was, too.

We didn't do that, though. The boys rode off on their bicycles, and Maggie Rose sat on the living room floor to play with her Legos. Legos are not very interesting toys because I am not allowed to chew them. That isn't to say I don't try every so often, but it makes my girl sad, so I tried to remember to leave the Legos alone and attack one of my other toys instead.

I decided to see what Mom was doing, so I went to the dining room. She was sitting at the table there, looking at her computer and tapping the keys. People like to do this a lot, even though computers do not smell interesting at all.

I sat under the table. I couldn't smell any

food up there, but I'd had a lot of luck under that table in the past. I lay there patiently but got up when Dad opened the door and walked in. I wagged and pawed his leg, and he petted me.

Getting a full dog greeting is probably one of the things humans like best about walking in the door, so I make sure everyone in the family knows they are loved as soon as they get home.

"What are you looking at?" Dad asked as he gave Mom a kiss.

Mom laughed softly. "I told you about those pigs we just rescued, remember?"

"They're so cute, Dad!" Maggie Rose called out from the living room.

"So I asked the manager who'd called me to send over his surveillance tapes so I could figure out how the pigs wound up inside an interstate truck stop," Mom went on. "Okay, watch this."

Maggie Rose went over to look at Mom's computer, too. She giggled, and Dad laughed, so I wagged.

"The two of them just walked up to the doors like they had an appointment!" Dad marveled. "That's amazing! Where'd they come from?"

"That's the mystery," Mom said. "Watch, here's another angle showing the entire parking lot."

I yawned sleepily, wondering if we'd all play something more exciting soon. I gnawed on Maggie Rose's shoelace, just to pass the time.

"Okay, see," Mom continued. "We've got the parking lot, plus just a little bit of the interstate on the other side. Now watch."

I looked up curiously when Maggie Rose gasped.

"Wait, what just happened?" Dad said.

"First there were no pigs, and then all of a sudden, there they are at the truck stop."

Mom turned and looked at him. "I know. It's as if they appeared by magic. I don't think they crossed that highway, but what else can explain it? And how would they have gotten onto the highway in the first place? I figured they must be from a farm in the area, but I checked and there are no hog farms anywhere nearby, so that's not it. Yet these little girls are *babies*—no way they came from miles away."

"I'm stumped," Dad admitted. "I don't know what to think."

"Well, either way, they're here now. Those piglets are going to wake up very hungry. I've already told our supplier that we need a *lot* of goat milk."

"You're telling me they eat like pigs," Dad said with a chuckle. I wagged at the laughter.

"I'm telling you every two hours, twenty-four hours a day, for at least the next several days," Mom replied.

"Every *two hours*? All night long? Are you serious?"

"Welcome to animal rescue," she said.

"I'll help!" Maggie Rose said eagerly.

Mom smiled. "I know you will, sweetie. But we're going to need the whole family to make this work."

"Huh. Actually," Dad replied, "I was thinking of driving up to Evergreen to see if I can spot that black bear people have been talking about."

"Oh, *really*?" Mom said. "You're going to do that and also help feed the pigs?"

"Um," Dad answered slowly. "I sort of thought if I wasn't here, you'd be the one to feed them all night."

"Do you remember, James," Mom responded lightly, "when I had to get up in the middle of the night to be with our newborn babies? You said you couldn't do it because it was the 'mom's job.'"

"Why do I get the feeling you're never going to let me forget that?" Dad replied.

Maggie Rose giggled.

Mom reached into a bag on the table next to her and pulled out two glass bottles. "Well," she said cheerfully, "I've decided that feeding pigs is a dad's job."

Dad picked up one of the glass bottles and held it with a funny look on his face while Maggie Rose laughed so hard she fell down, and I got to jump on her and lick her face and chew on her hair. At last, we were playing something fun!

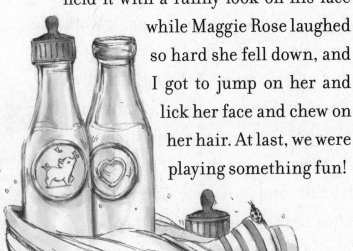

T hat night was the best! Dad and Maggie Rose and I stayed overnight at Work. I had never done that before. I was so excited!

At Work, most of the animals live in cages or kennels. I'm the only one who gets to be out, roaming around, sniffing and greeting all my old friends and any new arrivals. Most of the animals don't stay at Work too long—they leave after a few days or weeks, usually when a happy person or a family full of happy people comes to get them.

I'm sad to see my friends leave Work, but they and the people are so happy it makes up for it. Plus, there are always new friends to get to know.

That night, Brewster, the old dog who mostly takes naps, came out to sleep with me on a blanket.

Maggie Rose stretched out on a mat on the floor, while Dad lay down on the narrow bed

where Maggie Rose sometimes lies down to read her books when she comes to Work.

The pigs, however, hardly slept at all. They squealed and snorted, and when Dad picked up one of them and pushed a bottle into her mouth, the delicious aroma of warm milk filled the air. Brewster and I would look at each other with bewildered expressions. Why did pigs get milk while there was none for dogs? What was going on here?

While one pig was beingfed, the other one raced around on the floor, diving under Dad's bed, leaping up on top of me and

Brewster, making Maggie Rose laugh, and just generally going completely pig.

They were fantastic playmates. They loved to play Chase-Me, whether they were tearing after me or each other or running away from me when it was my turn to chase.

Dad would lie back on his bed, and the pigs would dart over to him and squeal to make sure he was paying attention to them. They were locked out of the big room where most of the animals slept in their cages, so they ran around and around the room where we were playing and tipped over a small table and bashed into a shelf and crashed into some chairs.

Brewster slept through most of this and was very grumpy when one of the pigs jumped on him. This happened many times. Brewster kept staring at me as if he thought I should do something to make the pigs behave.

Why would I, when we were all having so much fun?

Dad never took a bottle and gave me milk, but he sure enjoyed doing that with the pigs. Maggie Rose did it, too. After a while, though, she lay down on her mat and closed her eyes and stayed there, and Dad fed both of the pigs.

Again and again, I'd look over to see him holding one or the other in his lap, feeding them, his eyes half-closed.

"I can't believe I have to do this again so soon, Lily," Dad said with a sigh. I wondered if he was telling me how much fun we were having at Work all night long. "How can they eat so much?"

I heard the question and did Sit. What else could I do under the circumstances?

At one point, the two wiggly pigs curled up against Brewster's warm side.

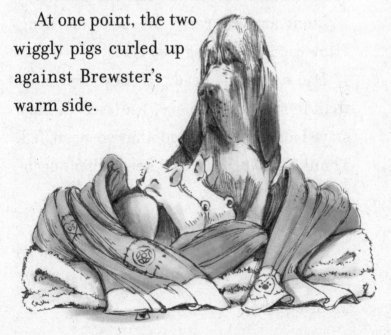

I lay down with Maggie Rose, and Dad flopped back on his bed, and I thought we were all going to sleep for a good long time.

I was wrong, though, because pretty soon, the pigs started squealing again. Maggie Rose didn't stir, but Brewster picked up his head and snorted, and Dad had both hands over his eyes. "No. No, please," he begged.

I wagged. Dad fed the pigs some more. It seemed to be his new favorite thing to do.

Mom arrived early the next morning. "How did it go?" she asked Dad.

Dad shook his head. "If they slept more than ten minutes apiece, I missed it, but I stayed on schedule and they've been fed. Thank God for Lily. She keeps them occupied."

I wagged because he'd said my name.

"I'll take over feeding them. Will you go home and get the kids some breakfast?" Mom asked.

"Sure," Dad agreed. "And then I'm going to bed. Today, Dad's job is to take a nap."

I woke up Maggie Rose by licking her ears, and we left Work and went home. The rest of my family was seated at the table. Craig fed me some eggs, and Maggie Rose told me I was a good dog.

After we ate, Craig and Bryan went

57

outside, Maggie Rose lay down with a book, and Dad did something very curious—he climbed into his bed. I had never seen him go back to bed in the middle of the day before!

I was tired from chasing pigs all night and wondered if he would let me climb up to be with him.

He did.

Everything was different now that I had two pig friends at Work. Maggie Rose gave them names; the fast one was called Scamper, and the really fast one was called Dash. Scamper and Dash spent all of their time either lying in people's laps being given milk from bottles, skittering around Work like crazy playing Chase-Me, getting me to play Chase-Me-I'm-a-Pig, or sleeping.

They went into their naps like they did everything else: with a crash. One moment they would be careening around, sliding and squealing, and the next they would be collapsed in a pile of pig, eyes shut, noses twitching.

When I wanted to nap, I usually went to find Brewster. I like the way Brewster settles down for a doze. He paws at his bed, getting it properly rumpled up, turns around a few times, and then lies heavily down.

And when he wakes up, he does it properly, yawning and stretching and scratching himself and then lying around getting used to the idea of being awake. The pigs, on the other hand, woke up on the run. They would be completely still one moment and doing Chase-Me an instant later.

I got to go to Work most nights, which was amazing! Sometimes I'd be there with Mom, sometimes with Dad. Every now and then, Bryan or Craig or Maggie Rose would come, too. I loved that!

The people didn't seem as happy as I was, though.

"When is this going to end?" Craig groaned at one point.

"I'm tired," Bryan agreed, holding Dash in his lap. "This is boring."

"I'll do it," Maggie Rose said. Bryan gave Dash to her.

"Animal rescue isn't always about cuddling puppies and kittens," Mom told us. "It's hard work. But think what we've done. These little girl piggies wouldn't survive if it weren't for us."

"And Lily!" my girl chimed.

"And Lily," Mom agreed.

I wagged, though no treats resulted from all this talk about me.

Now, I loved my new pig friends. They were fun to play with. But I did not see why no one thought that a good dog should be given milk from a bottle, since that was what we were doing with Scamper and Dash.

Brewster wasn't fed any milk, either, but

he didn't seem to care about that. What he did care about was how the pigs would run over and jump on him. He did not seem to like it. He didn't growl, but he did groan a lot. I tried to herd the pigs away from Brewster when I could.

"This is killing me," Dad complained one day.

We had been at Work all day. Now Brewster was deep into a nap, and I was watching jealously as Mom and Dad sat in chairs and gave the little pigs a meal.

"It's killing us," Mom corrected tiredly. "They have so much energy!"

"I think we need to get these little girls feeding on their own," Dad said. "I can't do this much longer, and you've got other animals to take care of at the rescue."

"You're right," Mom replied resignedly. "They're for sure old enough to feed themselves, but I don't know what to do. I put goat milk in a bowl, but they weren't at all interested. I think they prefer being bottle-fed. It makes them feel loved."

Mom's phone jangled in her pocket, and she reached in awkwardly and held it up to her ear. "Hello?" she said sleepily.

Then she sat bolt upright and didn't seem to notice as the bottle slipped out of Dash's mouth.

"Oh no," she said. "Oh, goodness! I'll be right there." She got up and dumped Dash in Dad's lap.

"What happened?" Dad asked. He looked worried. I sat up, watching both of their faces intently in case they needed my help.

"That was the school," Mom said. "Maggie Rose fell asleep in class, and she slid right out of her chair onto the floor."

I heard my girl's name and gazed around alertly for her, but I didn't see or smell her anywhere near.

Dad and Mom looked at each other.

"You'd better go get her," Dad said with a sigh. He looked down at the pigs in his lap. "When you're back, we'll figure out something to do."

Mom left, and Dad finished feeding Scamper and Dash. We all played Chase-Me until Mom came back again. She had my girl with her! Maggie Rose!

I ran to my girl and greeted her with my tail wiggling back and forth. I licked her knees and her hands when she reached down to scratch me.

Mom and Dad seemed to think that Maggie Rose needed a lot of attention, too. They fussed over her until they got her settled on the long, narrow bed where Dad sometimes lay down when we were doing Work at night, feeding the pigs and playing Chase-Me.

"But I'm not sick or anything!" Maggie Rose said. "I just got sleepy."

"Lie right there and close your eyes," Mom said. "You're going to take a nice long nap. And no more overnights at the rescue for you. That's final."

"But who's going to help feed the pigs?" Maggie Rose asked. She sounded worried. I jumped up onto the skinny bed with her and snuggled up against her so she'd know I'd always take care of her.

Mom sighed. "We'll figure it out. Right now, rest."

"Can I have my snack from school first?" Maggie Rose asked. "I'm hungry."

Maggie Rose had put down her backpack next to the bed. Mom unzipped it and reached in and pulled out a crinkly bag and handed it to Maggie Rose.

I sat up with my ears perked high. Crinkly bags are excellent for having treats in them!

Sure enough, Maggie Rose began taking things out of the bag and putting them in her mouth. I sniffed but could not smell anything particularly delicious.

"Want a blueberry, Lily?" Maggie Rose asked me. She held out her hand. There was a small dark fruit in her palm, but it did not interest me.

The two pigs ran over to see what we were doing. They couldn't jump up on the couch like me, but they stretched their necks as high as they could. Their little snouts were twitching like mad. "Hey, Mom," Maggie Rose asked, "can I feed Scamper and Dash some blueberries?"

Mom and Dad glanced at each other. "Sure, why not?" Mom agreed.

My girl held out fruits in each hand, one for Scamper, and one for Dash. The pigs shoved their mouths right into her open palms and scarfed them up. Maggie Rose laughed. "They love blueberries!" she sang.

Mom stood and walked over. Scamper and Dash were not doing Sit because they were pigs and not dogs, but they were trying to do something like it with their eyes, staring up at my girl eagerly.

"Do you think I could have some of those blueberries?" Mom asked.

Maggie Rose handed over the crinkly bag that had been so disappointing to me. Mom went to the refrigerator and pulled out a bottle. The refrigerator at home has wonderful smells that charge out into the room every time the door is open, but the one here at Work is much less interesting.

I perked up when I caught the scent of what Mom was pouring into the bowl on the counter. It was some of that rich, fragrant milk that the pigs were always eating. Food in a bottle might be for Scamper and Dash, but food in a bowl was for a good dog!

Scamper and Dash must have known this because they turned and headed out the door and down the hall, probably to jump on Brewster or knock over some furniture.

I was disappointed to see Mom toss some of Maggie Rose's fruits into my bowl of milk. I decided, though, that I could lap up the milk and leave the little fruits. This is just one of the things dogs must learn to do.

"Maggie Rose," Mom said. "Can you hold on to Lily for just a moment?"

I heard my name and figured that Mom was telling my girl that I was finally about to be fed some of the delicious milk. Then Maggie Rose wrapped her arms around me, holding me on her lap. That was a strange thing to do, because now I couldn't get at the bowlful of milk!

"Good dog," my girl said to me.

Good dog? *Good dog?* What happened next was not the sort of thing that should happen to a good dog!

"Okay!" Mom said. "Scamper! Dash! Come have some breakfast."

My new pig friends had learned their names a little bit and came racing into the room, either because Mom had called them or because they just felt like it.

That's how they did things. They were not like dogs, who must pay attention to what people want. They were just crazy pigs, who thought their job should be to run around and then have milk even though a good dog doesn't get any.

Mom put the big bowl down on the floor, and I naturally surged forward, but my girl's hands held me still. What were we doing?

Scamper and Dash shoved their noses

into my dog bowl. Milk went flying everywhere, and my pig friends started to eat my treat! What were they doing?

"The blueberries worked!" Mom exclaimed.

Dad was smiling. "This could change our lives forever," he said with a laugh. "No more bottle-feeding around the clock!"

I did not understand why Mom and Dad seemed so happy when right in front of their eyes these pigs were taking my treat.

"They love blueberries," Maggie Rose said with a cheerful grin.

I looked at her in dismay. She did not seem at all unhappy that these pigs were busily making sure that I would not get any milk from my bowl.

Soon, Scamper and Dash were done ruining my morning and took off running again. Maggie Rose released me, and I went over and sniffed the bowl, licking up a few drops of milk that were splattered on the floor. It was as delicious as I had supposed.

I mournfully examined the now clean bowl, smelling the remnants of some of Maggie Rose's fruits as well the faintest hint of my milk, all gone to the pigs.

That night at dinner, I sprawled forlornly under the table, thinking about how wonderful it would have been to have my milk. Mom said both pigs' names, and I figured that was what the family was discussing: how Scamper and Dash had gobbled up my food by mistake while Maggie Rose forgot to let go of me.

"I have that appointment up in the foothills tomorrow," Dad said. "I'll take Maggie Rose and Lily with me." I raised my head at my name but otherwise didn't react. There really was nothing surprising to me about the fact that everyone was sitting at the dinner table discussing what a good dog I am.

"From what you said about the ranch, it seems promising," Mom replied.

"Can I go?" Bryan asked.

"You boys both have soccer," Mom replied.

"Is it a pig ranch?" Maggie Rose asked.

"No," Dad said. "But it might work out for Scamper and Dash. The rancher wants their manure for his compost. Up in the hills, it's tough to get a good compost heap going because it's so dry. If they try to add food scraps, it'll just attract raccoons or other scavengers."

"What's compost?" Maggie Rose asked.

"Oh, it's stuff like dead leaves or grass clippings and leftover food and animal manure, too," Dad replied. "It'll become natural fertilizer if you let it rot in just the right way. So Scamper and Dash can help with that.

"He says he's got an electrified, fenced-in pen that he can move each day for them. They'll do what pigs do, which is to churn the soil underneath their feet. Pigs love to wallow in mud. So it'll be good for everyone— at least, that's what he claims. We'll have to see."

6

The next day, we took Scamper and Dash for a car ride!

Dad drove. Maggie Rose and I sat in the back seat, where I could keep an eye on the pigs who were in their cage in the far back. They made a lot of squealing noises when we first started driving, but then they settled down for a nap.

They liked to sleep on top of each other, and I noticed that when Scamper twitched her ears, Dash twitched her ears at exactly the same time. This is not something dogs do. If I move my ears, Brewster doesn't move his.

Was this why the pigs were given milk and I wasn't? Did my human family think that twitching ears deserved a treat, just like Maggie Rose gives me a treat for doing Roll Over?

It is hard to tell what people are thinking sometimes. Ear twitching didn't seem like much of a trick, but then again, neither did Roll Over, when I thought about it.

We drove for some time, and I figured we were headed back to where I'd first met my little pig friends, a place with food smells and clothing hanging down for Bryan and Craig to push over. Instead, we wound up at a spot that smelled powerfully of cows and horses.

We parked in the shade of a large tree, and Maggie Rose and Dad and I jumped out. Scamper and Dash had woken up, but they stayed where they were, lifting their noses inside their cage.

A man in dusty clothing came over and held out his hand. "It's nice to meet you, Mr. Cleveland," Dad told him. "I'm James Murphy. This is my daughter, Maggie Rose."

"Call me Owen," the man replied.

My nose was up and twitching like mad. I could smell animals, but I could not see any.

"I'm sure glad you're here," the man in dusty pants said. "My boy found an abandoned fawn, and we were thinking we needed to call somebody, and then I remembered that I was getting a visit from a game warden today." I felt Dad stiffen, and Maggie Rose and I both glanced at him curiously.

"Did you touch it?" Dad asked.

Dirty Pants Man shook his head. "Nope, but she's clearly starving."

"I need to see it right now," Dad said. "Can you take me to it?"

Maggie Rose put my leash on my collar. Dad opened the back of our truck, lifted out the cage, and set Scamper and Dash on the ground in the shade. They charged up to the door and looked like they were waiting to get out and run around.

Dad, however, did not let them out. This

was a time for dogs, not pigs, to walk with people.

We followed the man across some ground toward a stand of lush trees. His clothing gave off clouds of dust as he walked.

That's when I saw the horses standing at a fence and staring at us. They seemed surprised that there could be anything so wonderful as a dog visiting their home. I wanted to trot over and sniff them and say hello, but my job was to be with my girl, and she was with Dad.

"What do we do, Dad?" Maggie Rose asked. "If the deer is starving?"

Dad rubbed his jaw. "Well, a doe will leave a newborn fawn alone by itself for as much as twelve hours at a time. I suspect that we're not dealing with a starving animal, probably just a newborn who hasn't yet fed enough to get any meat on her bones."

I think I was probably the first one to

smell it: a new creature, female, young, furry but not a dog. I had met an animal who smelled like this once before, something with long legs that Dad had called a *deer*.

The man with the dirty pants slowed, crouched, and pointed. I guessed that he could smell the deer, too. "See? Right there, under that tree."

I could see the thing now. It was small, a little smaller than I am. It had big dark eyes and ears that stuck out from its head. It wasn't moving at all—like a dog who has been told to do Stay.

Painted over this foreign creature's scent was another smell, the same sort of animal, but different—bigger, older. Also, I could detect an odd, faint, milky odor as well.

It reminded me of when Scamper and Dash would climb on top of Brewster and irritate him out of his nap. After they had roused him, the pigs would smell a tiny bit like Brewster, and he would smell a tiny bit like them. That's what I supposed might have happened here. This small deer had been napping with another, older one.

That did not explain the milk, though. Perhaps earlier, Dirty Pants Man had been here with a bottle of milk. It was discouraging to think that all these animals were being given milk but a dog wasn't.

See?" Dirty Pants Man whispered. "The poor thing is like to starving."

"No," Dad replied. "It's what I'd thought:

this fawn was just born yesterday. Its mother left it here to go forage. In fact, I wouldn't be surprised if she's very close by, watching us."

As we were sitting there, I picked up a new hint of the odor that was on the little deer. The animal that had been lying with it was somewhere over in a deeper stand of trees. I looked and could not see it, but I sure could smell it! The milk odor was also stronger, too, now that I knew to sniff for it.

"So the baby deer is okay, Dad?" Maggie Rose asked.

"Yes," Dad replied. "All we need to do is leave it alone. Its mother will take care of the rest."

Dad straightened up, and that's when I caught the faintest movement. There it was—a bigger deer, just like the small one except for its size. It was staring at us without moving a muscle. Maybe it was like

Brewster and didn't like to move any more than it had to.

Dirty Pants Man smiled. "Well, you learn something new every day," he said. "I for sure thought I needed to help it."

"Don't worry, this happens all the time," Dad replied. "People mean well, and when they see a newborn fawn, they think it must be abandoned because they're so skinny and aren't moving, as if they're too weak to stand up. But that's their instinct. The fawn couldn't possibly run away from predators, so all it can do is lie still and hope nothing spots it. Often, people bring a baby deer to us at the wildlife refuge, but it's very hard to raise them by hand. It's almost always best to leave them where they are."

We were done looking at the little creature and smelling the other one in the woods, because we turned away and headed back. The man with the dusty pants walked with us to our truck.

"So, don't you think this would be a good place for your rescue piglets?" the man asked.

"Well, that depends," Dad replied.

I did Sit because apparently Dad and Dirty Pants Man were planning to talk for a while.

"See," Dad explained, "I didn't realize you were so close to the foothills. Probably a lot of predators up there that might come down if they pick up the scent of pigs. Does your portable cage have a lid on it?"

"A lid?" the man replied slowly. "Nope,

didn't think I'd need one. They aren't *flying* pigs, are they?"

The men laughed.

Maggie Rose spoke up. "The lid is to keep out animals that can climb, like mountain lions. And eagles, even, if the pigs are little."

"That's my game warden girl," Dad said with a smile. "She's absolutely right."

The man shook his head. "Too bad. Well, I hope you find these little ladies a good home."

Dad picked up the cage with the little pigs in it and put it in the truck. Maggie Rose and I and Dad got in, but the man with the dirty pants did not, so he probably didn't want to take a car ride with a couple of pigs in the back.

"Well, I do appreciate you setting me straight about that little fawn. I thought it was starving for sure," he told us.

"You're welcome," Dad replied.

Dad started the truck, and with a wave from my girl, we all drove away.

"You were absolutely right about the cage, Maggie Rose," Dad said. "I bet Mr. Cleveland doesn't think about predators because he mostly has horses and cows. Mountain lions won't attack a herd of big animals unless they're desperate, and both horses and cows can protect their young. But Scamper and Dash are almost defenseless."

"We can't let anything happen to the pigs," Maggie Rose declared firmly.

"I know, Maggie Rose. There's another rancher who responded to our posting," Dad said. "We're headed there now. Maybe he'll have a better situation."

I grew sleepy as we drove, but I was unable to nap because Scamper and Dash kept squealing and jumping around in their cage.

We stopped again at a new place and got

out. It smelled a lot like where we had just been. There was the distinct odor of horses on the air, and I saw a few of them walking in the grass.

Horses do not know how to play fun games the way dogs do. I have never seen one chase a ball or wrestle with others in the park. All they do is stand around and look at one another or at the grass they are chewing on. One dog is more fun than all the horses I've ever seen in my life put together.

A man came out of his house as Dad lifted out the cage with the pigs in it and put it on the ground again. Next to the man, there was a boy who looked like he was Maggie Rose's age.

The boy ran up to us and then stopped. "Hi."

Maggie Rose looked at the ground for a moment, maybe trying to figure out what it was that horses found so fascinating about grass. "Hi," she said.

"My name's Bobby," the boy told her.

"I'm Maggie Rose," my girl said.

"Huh," the boy replied. "Is Rose your last name, or is that your middle name?"

"My middle name. I'm Maggie Rose Murphy," Maggie Rose said.

"Well, I'm Bobby Jacob Dell," the boy replied.

I could see this was going to be one of those times when people stood around talking for a long while. When that happens, all a good dog can do is either wait for them to play or go off on her own. Since I was off leash, I had wandered away, sniffing at the bases of trees and along the tires of our truck, when I saw something overhead. It was Casey the crow, my best friend!

Casey likes to follow me around and land

on my back. Lately, he had started chasing us when we did Car Ride in the truck.

He turned lazy circles overhead before fluttering down on a tree branch just above the cage where Scamper and Dash were busily wrestling with each other.

And that's when I smelled it: a very familiar scent was coming to me on the breeze.

Frankly, it smelled a lot like Scamper and Dash, so I knew instantly that it was pig. In that moment, I recalled the big animal watching us as the baby animal lay on the ground. There had been a milk smell on the large creature, and I now understood that it was the mother of the little animal in the grass.

That's why the two animals' scents had been mingled. The mother had been lying with the little animal. Mothers do that sort of thing. My mother used to, in the time when I lived with her and not with Maggie Rose.

This made me remember something else. When I first met Scamper and Dash, they had been coated with a thick blanket of odor. It had smelled like grown-up pig and also a little bit like milk.

Obviously, what I had smelled on Scamper and Dash was a mother smell. Scamper and Dash had a mother! And the familiar odor coming to me now was that very same pig.

I do not know if the two little pigs smelled their mother, but I sure did. I went to the cage, and we touched noses. Scamper and Dash were, as usual, full of energy and wanting to race around even inside the small cage. If I were in there, we would all be wrestling.

I knew if I wanted to be a really good friend to them, I would lead them toward that mother scent.

When animals are very young, they need to be with their mothers. I used to be with mine. Even though I had to share her with too many brothers, I loved being near her.

I didn't need my mother anymore, because I had Maggie Rose now. But the little pigs were different. They were younger than I was. And they didn't have their own people yet, the way I had my girl.

If the little pigs were going to reach their mother, they needed to come out of the cage.

I pawed at the cage door, frustrated that it was locked. I looked over at my girl to see if she was willing to come help me. However, she was busy talking to the boy her age while Dad was busy talking to the man his age. I would have to help my friends on my own.

I pawed at the door again, and the pigs watched curiously. They did not know what I was doing, but they were very interested in it, anyway.

With a flutter, Casey the crow landed on the bars at the top of the cage. This was very exciting to the two pigs, who raced around in small circles and then jumped on each other.

Casey was watching me, though, not the pigs. He twisted his head one way and the other, in a gesture that I had learned meant that he was trying to figure something out.

I raised my paw to the cage door again. The crow spread his wings and lifted himself off the top of the cage and landed right on my head!

I sat and held still, because Casey doesn't like it when I run around with him up there. The two pigs looked absolutely dumbfounded to see a bird on a dog's head. I waited patiently to see what Casey would do next.

Casey fluttered up off me and pecked at the cage door, gripping the wires with his feet so that he hung there, going *peck, peck, peck.* I watched as he did this for what seemed a long time. Then suddenly, with a rattle, the cage door opened!

Instantly, Scamper and Dash charged out, so thrilled to be free that they were paying absolutely no attention to where they were running. I watched as they vanished around the corner of the house, and then I took off in pursuit.

8

Scamper and Dash are very fast, but I was able to catch up with them. As soon as I did, their game shifted from Let's-Chase-Small-Pigs to Let's-Chase-Lily!

I could smell the scent of the mother pig as clearly as anything I had ever smelled. Since the two little pigs were already chasing me, I turned and ran straight for some trees, tracking the scent as if it were a trail in the dirt. Scamper and Dash instantly followed.

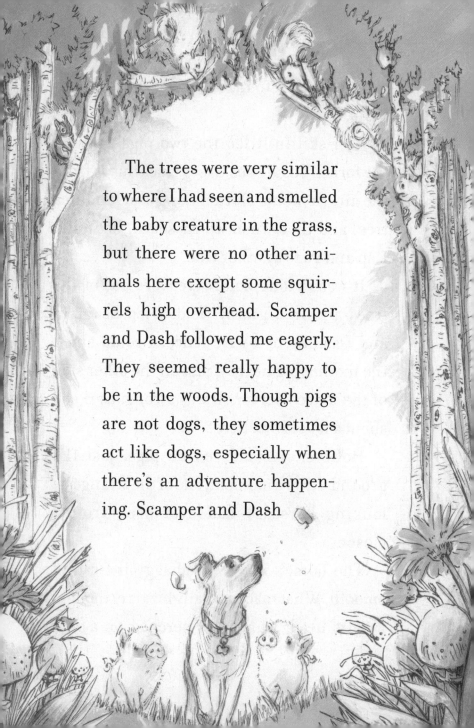

The trees were very similar to where I had seen and smelled the baby creature in the grass, but there were no other animals here except some squirrels high overhead. Scamper and Dash followed me eagerly. They seemed really happy to be in the woods. Though pigs are not dogs, they sometimes act like dogs, especially when there's an adventure happening. Scamper and Dash were as excited to race through the woods as I was.

As I skillfully led the two pigs through the forest, I could see Casey tracking us from the air. He would flutter along and land in a tree, and then when we passed it, he would flap and go to another tree.

It wasn't long before we were out of the trees and in a grassy field. I led Scamper and Dash up to a wire fence. I could smell the mother pig nearby, just on the other side of the fence. Her smell was strong, as if she spent a lot of time here.

However, I could see no pigs, just flat ground. After a moment, one of the strangest-looking horses I had ever seen trotted closer.

The horse's body was shaggy instead of smooth. What made it really bizarre, though, was its head, which was perched on a very long neck. Most horses have ridiculously large heads, with huge noses. This horse-thing had a face more like a dog's and ears that stuck straight up.

The horse creature spotted me and came directly over to where Scamper, Dash, and I were huddled near the fence. I did not know if I should bark or not. The horse-thing was odd, but it didn't seem to be a threat. In fact, it seemed more curious than anything, gawking at me.

It was probably astounded to see an amazing dog and her pig friends.

After a time of staring at the horse creature and having it stare back, I heard a woman's voice. "What do you see?" the woman called.

I wagged as I saw a woman walking slowly across the field toward us. The odd horse turned its head to look at her.

"What is it?" the woman asked.

I decided that this horse creature couldn't talk any better than regular horses, or it would have responded by now.

All of a sudden, the woman clapped her

hands together. "Piggies!" she said, and she started moving very swiftly toward us. "Pig-gies!"

She was obviously happy to see me, which made sense, because I am a dog.

When she was very close, she turned to look back and put her fingers to her lips. There was a very loud, very shrill whistle. "Pig-pig-pig-pig!" she called in a high voice.

I wondered if she had a dog named Pig-pig-pig-pig.

But instead of a dog, a big, fat, pale-colored pig appeared around a corner of a house on the other side of the field. She came wad-dling toward us, and I knew at once that she was the pig I had been smelling since we had arrived! There was no longer a milk scent clinging to her, but she was definitely the source of the odor that had been painted all over Scamper and Dash the day I'd first met them.

My little pig friends began squealing. At the sound of their voices, the mother's trot broke into a full-out gallop—not a fast gallop, though. When animals get older, they don't move as quickly as Scamper and Dash. But I could tell that she was moving as swiftly as she could manage.

She raced toward us while the horse creature stood frozen, clearly not sure what was going on.

I honestly didn't understand everything myself. But the woman was now very close, and I knew that she would take charge the way people always do.

"Could it be?" the woman asked. I heard the question in her voice and wagged, thinking she was asking me if I was a good dog. Obviously, I was.

The woman was now right up to the fence, and the horse creature took a step back from

her. She reached a hand through the wires, and I licked it.

Then the mother pig arrived. My little pig friends went completely crazy, squealing and squawking and rubbing up against the wires and pressing their snouts at their mother.

Their mother was squealing, too. "Come on, pig," the woman urged. She began walking along the inside of the fence, and so I led Scamper and Dash in the same direction. Casey was watching from a nearby tree.

The horse creature decided to tag along with us because I was a dog and obviously knew what to do when things are confusing. There was a good long stretch of fence, but after a while, the woman came to a gate.

She pushed it open. My two pig friends burst past me and ran to their mother, so I followed.

The woman shut me into her yard with a clank of the gate.

"I don't understand how this happened," the woman marveled. "But these are your babies, aren't they, Sadie?" she asked the big pig.

Scamper and Dash were leaping all over their mother as if she were Brewster trying to take a nap. She was nuzzling them and making low, happy cries.

Just then, I heard a high voice coming from the direction of the trees. "Lily!" the voice called.

It was Maggie Rose.

ell, even though
my girl was yell-
ing for me, I couldn't run to her because I
was in a yard behind a fence! When I heard
Dad call my name, I barked. The moment I
barked, that horse creature regarded me in
absolute amazement.

A lot of animals are really impressed
when they hear a dog barking, as well they
should be.

I went to the gate and did Sit, being a good

dog, expecting the woman to open it, but she did not. I looked up in the air to see if Casey could fly down to help. He'd opened the pigs' cage, so he could probably open this gate, too.

But Casey was still in the trees and didn't seem to know I needed his aid.

Every time I heard Maggie Rose's voice calling my name, it sounded closer, and I joyously barked right back. Soon, I saw Dad and Maggie Rose emerge from the trees, their scents coming to me on the air.

"Lily!" Maggie Rose called again. She broke from Dad's side and ran up to the fence, so I was able to push my nose through the wire to touch her outstretched hand. "What are you doing here, Lily?" Maggie Rose asked.

Dad approached, peering at the big pig and the woman. He took off his cap and scratched his head. "Hello," he said to the woman. "Looks like you found our dog and our pigs."

Scamper and Dash were still joyously climbing all over their mother pig.

The woman was smiling. "Howdy," she said. "I'm hoping you'll be able to explain what just happened, because I'm pretty sure these are the same two little piglets that I

lost more than a week ago. At least, I think they are. And Sadie sure acts like they are."

The big pig had rolled onto her back, and the little pigs were all over her, still squealing and jumping around.

"They are? Well, my wife's rescue got a call that there were two little pigs loose in a truck stop off I-25. When she got there, these little girls were racing around, knocking over clothing racks, and having a grand old time, so she scooped them up and took them back to the animal rescue, and we bottle-fed them until they were old enough to eat on their own. Now we've been out looking for a home for them."

The woman shook her head. "I-25? Truck stop? I wasn't at a truck stop." Suddenly, she gasped. "Wait! I did stop at a rest area. And I think . . . Yes! There was a truck stop across the highway. Somehow these little girls wriggled their way out of the livestock trailer and must've crossed that highway. It's hard to believe, but there can't be any other explanation."

"We've been trying to find a good home for Scamper and Dash," Dad said. "That's what my little girl here named them." Maggie Rose looked up and smiled a little. "We were at your neighbor's place, and they somehow escaped their cage. Her dog, Lily, must have led the pigs straight to your ranch."

"Well, if you're looking for a good home, there isn't a better one than right here with their mommy," the woman said. "I have ducks in my pond, I have that llama, I've got a few cats and an old donkey, and I just love farm animals. I bought Sadie and her two little ones so that they could come here and have a happy life. Scamper and Dash? Those are fine names."

"Scamper is the one with the dark spot on her face," Maggie Rose said.

"I like this ranch," Dad observed. "I especially like the llama."

"Why do you have a llama?" Maggie Rose asked. "Do you ride it?"

"No," the woman replied. "Llamas are pack animals, so I suppose if I did a lot of camping up in the mountains, I'd take him with me and he'd carry my tent and supplies. But no, I just have him for safety."

"Safety?" Maggie Rose asked curiously.

"She's right, Maggie Rose," Dad said. "Llamas are protective. They watch out for their own young, but also for other animals who live with them. Especially a lone male like this one. If a predator showed up, the llama would run to attack it. They don't bite, really, but they can stomp with their legs, and they spit, too. Most predators will back off."

I noticed that my two pig friends had fallen fast asleep on their mother, who was

sprawled on the ground, lying on her side. It looked pretty cozy. I've never napped with a grown pig before, but I was starting to feel tempted.

"So," the woman said, "as you can see, this would be a good home. How much do you want for the pigs?"

"Oh no," Dad said. "I was never going to sell them. We were looking to adopt them out. I'm a game warden, but I spend almost as much time helping my wife's animal rescue as I do anything else. This is the first time we've had pigs, though."

"Well," the woman responded. "You must let me make a donation to your wife's rescue operation, at the very least."

Dad smiled. "That would be nice," he agreed.

"Could we come visit Scamper and Dash someday?" Maggie Rose asked. "It always makes me sad when we find a new home for an animal and I never get to see it again."

"Of course!" the woman said, grinning broadly. "I promise you Scamper and Dash will never forget you. And they'll definitely never forget your little dog!"

Maggie Rose walked over to where Sadie was lying sleepily with her dozing babies.

"Goodbye, Scamper," Maggie Rose said, giving Scamper a big hug. Dash opened her eyes and got to her feet so she wouldn't be left out.

"You, too, Dash," Maggie Rose said, hugging her as well.

We tracked back through the woods, following our scents. As we walked, I could not see or smell Casey anymore, and I wondered if he had flown back to be with Mom and Bryan and Craig.

When we returned to the truck, I saw that the boy and the man who had greeted us were no longer outside. The cage where Scamper and Dash had been wrestling still sat with its door open.

And there was Casey! He was inside the cage, watching us.

"Ree-ree," Casey croaked.

"He must have followed us somehow," Dad marveled. "But he doesn't want to fly all the way back. He wants a ride!" Dad put the cage with Casey in the back of the truck, and we slid in for the long car ride home. As soon as the car started moving, I climbed up and put my feet on the back of the seat so I could look at Casey.

I remembered the pigs. I remembered how happy they had been all the time, how fun it had been to have them with us. I understood now that they had found a new home back with their mother where they belonged. I did not know if I would ever see them again, but it had been wonderful to know them.

Casey was watching me, his head twisting from one side to the other.

I think he agreed.

MORE ABOUT PIGS

Pigs are quite smart. In experiments, they learned to play video games (using special joysticks) and to tell the difference between spearmint, peppermint, and mint. One particular group of pigs even learned to put all their toys away at the end of the day.

Piglets like to play. They chase each other, scamper about, toss their heads, and play-fight with other young pigs.

Pigs are actually quite clean. But they can't sweat to cool down, so they roll in mud to keep themselves from getting too hot. They will also huddle with other pigs to warm up.

Pigs don't lick themselves to keep clean, as dogs and cats do. Instead, they rub against something hard (like a tree, a rock, or a fence post) to scrape dirt off.

Pigs are easier to train than dogs or cats.

There are pigs on every continent of the world except Antarctica.

Pigs are not native to North and South America. Christopher Columbus brought the first pigs to this part of the world in 1493 when his ship landed in Cuba.

A female pig is a sow. A male pig is a boar.

A newborn pig is called a piglet. Mothers nurse their piglets for three to five weeks. Once a young pig is old enough to stop nursing it is known as a shoat.

Wild pigs live in a group called a sounder.

There are usually one to six sows and their children in a sounder.

Wild pigs eat mostly plants, including leaves, roots, berries, grass, seeds, or mushrooms. They will also eat worms, insects, and other small animals if they can get them. On farms, pigs usually eat corn or barley.

Pigs make nests to sleep in. Wild pigs use branches and grass. Farm pigs make piles of hay.

Pigs with curly tails may uncurl them when sleeping.

A pig's sense of smell is as keen as a dog's. Pigs can tell other pigs apart by smell.

Pigs are used to sniff out truffles, a rare and expensive fungus that grows underground.

© Ute Ville

W. BRUCE CAMERON is the *New York Times* bestselling author of *A Dog's Purpose*, *A Dog's Journey*, *A Dog's Way Home*, *A Dog's Promise*, and the young-reader novels *Bailey's Story*, *Ellie's Story*, *Lily's Story*, *Max's Story*, *Molly's Story*, *Shelby's Story*, and *Toby's Story*. He lives in California.

Don't miss this

LILY TO THE RESCUE

adventure!

W. BRUCE CAMERON

BESTSELLING AUTHOR OF
A DOG'S PURPOSE

LILY
TO THE rescue